Disney's
RECESS
THE JUNGLE GYM STANDOFF

Created by Joe Ansolabehere and Paul Germain

based on a television script by Joe Purdy

adaptation by Catherine McCafferty

illustrated by Christopher Nowell

 **A GOLDEN BOOK · NEW YORK**

Golden Books Publishing Company, Inc., New York, New York 10106

Rrrrrinnnngggg! The kids of Third Street School burst out the doors and raced toward Old Rusty. Their jungle gym definitely lived up to its name. Rusty patches and scratches covered its worn metal surface. A bare spot on the slide stopped kids cold halfway down. Still, all the kids felt the way T.J. did.

"Man," he said,
"I love this thing."

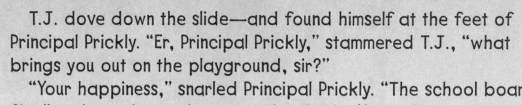

T.J. dove down the slide—and found himself at the feet of Principal Prickly. "Er, Principal Prickly," stammered T.J., "what brings you out on the playground, sir?"

"Your happiness," snarled Principal Prickly. "The school board's finally released some long-overdue funds. You kids are getting a brand-new, high-impact, plastic jungle gym!"

"YAAAAAAAY!" all the kids cheered.

"We'll just have to tear down this hunk of junk first," Principal Prickly added.

The cheering stopped. "You're gonna tear down Old Rusty?" asked Mikey in disbelief.

"That's right, kid," Prickly answered. "The construction workers will be here at eleven, so stay off it. And remember, if anyone asks, Principal Prickly's first priority is you children. Now get out of my way, you little brats!"

"I can't believe it," said T.J.
"Old Rusty was here when my
mom was in school," said Spinelli.

The bell rang, and T.J. watched the others wander sadly back to class.

"Aren't you coming?" Vince asked T.J.

"Naw, I think I'm just gonna play on Old Rusty a little longer." T.J. climbed to the top of the jungle gym. He sat there, thinking of all the fun times he and Old Rusty had shared.

T.J. was still sitting there at eleven o'clock, when the construction workers arrived.

"Hey, kid, what are you doing up there?" one worker called.

"Playing," T.J. answered.

"Well, get down!" the worker warned him.

But T.J. didn't move.

"Either you come down or we'll knock that thing down with you on it!" the impatient worker cried.

"If that's how I have to go, then so be it!" T.J. said bravely.

Grumbling, the construction workers entered the school building. A minute later, Miss Finster stormed out with them. Dozens of kids slipped out of the school behind her.

"T.J. Detweiler, get down from there this minute!" she shrieked.

"Never!" T.J. shouted back. "Old Rusty's the heart and soul of this school. He's almost as old as you are! Without Old Rusty, this place would just be a building with books and teachers and stuff!"

"Get down from there," Miss Finster shouted again, "or I'll come up there and get you myself!"

Everything got very quiet. Then suddenly a voice broke the silence. "Then you'll have to get me, too!" Mikey shouted as he climbed up to join T.J.

Soon the rest of the kids followed.
"Do something!" Miss Finster
sputtered to the construction workers.

"That's it!" bellowed Principal Prickly. "Miss Finster, execute Plan P."
Miss Finster rubbed her hands together in glee as the kids gasped.
"That's right," Principal Prickly told them, "I'm calling your parents!"

Soon traffic jammed the streets and driveway leading to the school. Parents followed Principal Prickly out to Old Rusty, where their kids swayed and sang.

"Look what your rotten, no-good children are up to!" said Prickly, pointing. "They've instigated a riot!"

But the parents weren't looking at their children. They were looking at Old Rusty, remembering all the fun they'd had there as kids.

"Your kids are standing in the way of progress," Principal Prickly told them. "Now get over there and do what you have to do!"

So the parents did just that. They joined their kids on Old Rusty's well-worn bars.

"All right, fine!" shouted Principal Prickly. "If they want to keep this rotten old pile of rust, let 'em! GO AHEAD AND KEEP IT!"

"We saved Old Rusty!" T.J. whooped. Kids, parents, and teachers alike cheered as Principal Prickly and Miss Finster headed back into the school.

Gretchen tugged on T.J.'s sleeve. "I've been doing some figuring," she began. "With this much weight on it—"

"What?" T.J. shouted. He couldn't hear her because there was too much shouting and cheering.

"There are too many people on—" Gretchen tried again.

But before she could finish, Old Rusty began to wobble.

"Look out! It's gonna cave!" shouted Spinelli, leaping to the ground. Everyone scrambled down the collapsing slide and off the bending bars.

Old Rusty crashed to the ground in a heap—and a cloud of rusty dust.

T.J. stared down at all the twisted metal. "After all that," he said, "and now it's gone."

A construction worker stepped forward and picked up a piece of Old Rusty. "Hey, Lou," he called to his partner, "doesn't the new model use these same kinds of parts?"

The other construction worker nodded as he took another piece from the pile. "Folks, leave it to us," he said.

When the builders were done, the school had a brand-new jungle gym. It looked just like Old Rusty!

T.J. stepped up to officially open the newly rebuilt jungle gym. "I christen you . . . New Rusty!" he proclaimed.

With a cheer, the kids swarmed
onto New Rusty.

One hundred years later, the recess bell rang. Students burst out the doors and raced toward New Rusty.

"Man," a kid said, "I love this thing."